GRIDIRON GAMER

Text by Thomas Kingsley Troupe
Illustrated by Fran Bueno

STONE ARCH BOOKS
a capstone imprint

Published by Stone Arch Books, an imprint of Capstone.
1710 Roe Crest Drive North Mankato, Minnesota 56003
capstonepub.com

Library of Congress Cataloging-in-Publication Data is
available on the Library of Congress website.
ISBN 9781666344660 (hardcover)
ISBN 9781666353327 (paperback)
ISBN 9781666344677 (ebook PDF)

Summary: Iako totally loves football. But being in a
wheelchair means he can never hit the real gridiron.
However, Iako makes up for it by being a whiz at
his favorite video game, *Football Blitz: Turbo*. When
his friends tell him he should play at a local esports
tournament, Iako hesitates. He doesn't think he's that
good. But when Iako plays a pickup game and beats
the current FB:T champion, he has a change of heart.
Iako decides to enter the tournament and prove he can
compete as well as anyone else. Will Iako's skills help
him defeat the current champ and claim the title?

Editor: Aaron Sautter
Designers: Brann Garvey, Elyse White
Production Specialist: Polly Fisher

Shutterstock: Elena_Lapshina,
(pixel texture) design element

TABLE OF CONTENTS

GRIDIRON LINEUP

LUZ

IAKO

CHAPTER 1

UNSTOPPABLE

The crowd cheered as quarterback Iako Tsantir unleashed a rocket of a pass. The football spun in a perfect spiral over the red-helmeted defenders, whistling toward the end zone.

There's no way this play will work, he thought, just before a West Virginia Warrior defensive end got to him. Iako held his breath as the two opposing cornerbacks were all over his receiver.

"Come on," Iako said to himself. "Come on."

As the ball got closer, the receiver jumped up, caught the ball, and juked to his left. The cornerbacks whiffed and slammed into each other. Iako's receiver ran the remaining five yards into the end zone.

"Touchdown!" Iako shouted in his bedroom, raising his game controller in the air. Sitting nearby, his best friend Darnell Peterson groaned. He fell back onto Iako's messy bed and tossed his controller aside.

"Seriously," Darnell said. "How are you so good at this?"

"C'mon, I'm not that good," Iako confessed. He watched his player on the screen do a victory dance while the crowd went bonkers.

Darnell sat up and hit the NEXT button on his controller. He didn't want to listen to the announcers talk about how great Iako's Florida Flamingos were.

"Hey," Iako said, "that's my favorite part!"

"Not sure why that would be," Darnell mumbled sarcastically. "You see it every few minutes or so."

Iako smiled. He'd been playing *FOOTBALL BLITZ: TURBO* nearly every day since the latest

version was released that spring. He'd gotten pretty good at it. He just wished he could play on his school's real football team like Darnell.

"Okay, c'mon, dude," Darnell said, pointing at the screen. "How are you doing that?"

Iako blinked a few times. "Sorry, I zoned out," he said. Then he noticed that he'd scored the extra point kick without even thinking about it.

"Exactly!" Darnell cried, pointing at the screen. "You're crushing me without even trying!"

"Let's watch that again," Iako said, selecting the INSTANT REPLAY option from the menu screen.

"Please, no," Darnell pleaded.

Iako and Darnell laughed as they rewound and watched the play again and again.

"Ugh! Stop tormenting me," Darnell said. "I can't take it anymore."

Iako smiled and punched his friend playfully in the shoulder. Darnell punched back.

"Hey, how dare you," Iako said with a smirk. "You can't hit a guy in a—"

"Five games in a row!" Darnell cut him off, holding up his hand. "FIVE. That's how I dare."

Iako shrugged. "Wanna make it six?"

Darnell shook his head and stood up. "I wish I could, but I need to get home for dinner."

"Tomorrow, then?" Iako asked. "I'll play as the worst team. That'll make it even, right?"

"Very funny," Darnell said, tossing his controller on the bed. "We'll have to see how I feel after football practice. I'm already tired and sore just thinking about Pain Week."

"Oh, that's right," Iako said. "Well, that sounds fun."

"You should play too," Darnell said. "There's all sorts of leagues you could get into."

Right, like that'll ever happen, Iako thought gloomily. He wished he could play real football.

"It's not for me, D," Iako replied, shutting off the game. "Besides, I don't really like big crowds."

"Mr. Introvert," Darnell sighed. "Well, I think you're missing out, man."

Iako nodded. "Yeah, probably."

The two friends bumped fists and said goodbye. After Darnell left, Iako sat quietly in his room. He daydreamed about how fun it would be to play with his best friend on the school's football team.

"Iakovos!" A voice called from the other end of the house. "It's dinner time!"

"Be right there, Mom!" Iako replied. He gripped the wheels of his wheelchair and pushed himself through the doorway.

CHAPTER 2

NO THANKS

The next day, Iako coasted along the hallway of Carter Valley Middle School and stopped near the large trophy case. Inside were all the trophies and plaques the school's sports teams had won during Carter Valley's 80-year history. There were few sports that the Carter Crocs weren't good at.

It felt weird being in school a week before summer was officially over. Iako guessed the fall sports coaches wanted to get an early start at practice.

As Iako waited for Darnell, he heard people coming out of the locker room. He looked up and saw a group of girls with damp hair, laughing and heading toward the door.

Swim team, Iako thought. *When are the football players done?*

A girl with dark, wet hair stopped near him and leaned up against the wall, looking at her phone.

"Are you waiting for a ride?" the girl asked.

"No," Iako said, patting the arms of his wheelchair. "I've got one."

The girl's eyebrows shot up and she grinned.

"Hey, that's pretty good," she said. "My name is Luz."

"Lose?" Iako said. "You mean, like the opposite of win?"

"You're hilarious," she replied. "No, it's Luz. Spelled L-U-Z, but pronounced lose. It's Spanish. My family is from Chile."

"Oh, cool," Iako said. "I'm Iako. Spelled I-A-K-O. But it's pronounced Yock-o. It's short for Iakovos," Iako explained. "My family's from Greece."

"Sounds like we've both got interesting names," Luz said with a snicker. "So is this school any good?"

"Sure," Iako said, nodding to the trophy case. "As you can see our sports teams are great."

Luz nodded and looked at the case. "Guess so," she said.

Iako shrugged. "Are you new to Carter Valley?" he asked.

"Yeah," Luz replied. "Always fun to start middle school in a new town where you don't know anybody."

"Ah," Iako said with a wave. "You'll be fine. People are pretty cool around here."

Luz smiled and nodded to the wheelchair.

"If you don't mind me asking," she began, "what happened? How'd you end up—"

"In this sweet set of wheels?" Iako cut in, admiring his own wheelchair. "I thought you'd never ask."

"Sorry," Luz replied. "It's not really my business. I just wondered if you were in an accident or something."

Iako shook his head. "It's fine, seriously. I've got muscular dystrophy. I was born with it. My legs are weak now, but in time it'll affect the rest of my body."

Luz shook her head. "Oh wow, I'm sorry."

Iako smiled. "Thanks, but I'm okay."

Then the sound of people laughing echoed down the hallway. Iako turned to see Darnell and a handful of football players heading out of the locker room. As soon as Darnell saw Iako, he groaned and covered his face.

"Dude, you're seriously waiting for me?" Darnell asked, stopping to bump fists with his friend.

"I was in the neighborhood," Iako shrugged. "Hey, this is Luz."

"Hi," Luz said.

"Lose?" Darnell said. "What kind of name is that?"

"Don't you start with me too," Luz said. "Hi, nice to meet you."

"Darnell," he replied. "Did Iako tell you how good of a football player he is? I'm sure he's here to embarrass me on the gridiron."

Luz turned to Iako with a confused look.

"*FOOTBALL BLITZ: TURBO,*" Iako replied. "It's a video game."

"Ah," Luz said. "My little brother plays that. He's mad that he can't sign up for the esports tournament coming up. He's too young."

Darnell smacked Iako's shoulder. "There you go, big shot. You could enter and show those guys who's boss."

Iako shook his head. "No thanks," he replied. "I don't like crowds. I just like to play against friends."

"Are you really that good?" Luz asked. Then she turned to Darnell. "Is he really good?"

"I'm not," Iako answered first.

"He *is*," Darnell said, correcting his friend. "*Ridiculously* good."

Luz raised her phone and quickly looked at it.

"Shoot," she said. "My ride is here. Nice meeting you two."

As Luz walked away, she glanced over her shoulder.

"You should think about that tournament, Iako," she said. "Might as well show the world what you can do."

Iako waved and Darnell did too. When she was gone, he turned to his friend.

"She seems cool," Darnell said. "But is her name really Lose?"

CHAPTER 3

RETIRED

After lunch, Iako and Darnell sat in Iako's room and loaded up *FOOTBALL BLITZ: TURBO* on his game console.

"You ready?" Iako asked.

Darnell looked over his team's stats on the TV. He was set to play as the Los Angeles Leopards. It was widely considered one of the best teams, both in the real world and in the video game version. He'd even added Hall of Fame quarterback Rick Armstrong.

"Yup, all set. I've got Armstrong starting," Darnell said.

"And I'm playing as the Rhode Island Rats," Iako said. "It's the new team with the worst stats ever."

"I can't lose!" Darnell said, nodding and getting himself pumped up to play.

Iako pressed the START BUTTON on his controller to get the game going.

They both smiled as the game announcer explained the match up for the players. Things looked good for Darnell at the start. His team won the coin flip, and he launched an offense that had Iako's defense scrambling to keep up. With speed and strength stats through the roof, it took three defenders to stop the Leopards' star running back.

"Okay, champ," Darnell shouted. "I've got you where I want you."

Iako watched the Leopards slice through his defense like they were a Pee-Wee team made up of 5-year-olds. By half time, Darnell was leading 21–3.

"Yeah, these guys are terrible," Iako said. "This is almost embarrassing."

"Now you know how I feel!" Darnell said. "Armstrong's arm does not disappoint!"

Iako nodded. It was going to take some serious work to come back, especially with a scrappy team like the Rhode Island Rats.

But then, halfway through the third quarter, something happened. Iako selected his left defensive end and blitzed Armstrong. Before Darnell knew what happened, his star quarterback was sacked, and the ball was knocked loose.

"Fumble!" Iako shouted.

He quickly switched control to his right tackle player, who scooped up the ball and ran it down the field. Although the Leopards were fast with their maxed-out stats, they couldn't catch up. As the Rats player crossed the end zone, he was tackled.

"Touchdown!" the game announcer cried.

"You've got to be kidding!" Darnell shouted.

He took a deep breath and shook it off. "It's okay, I still have the lead. I can still take you down."

But Darnell didn't. After making the extra point, Iako began to rally his team. In the fourth quarter, Iako intercepted a beautiful Armstrong pass. Then he inched the Rats downfield with a series of two to three yard plays. As time ran out, Darnell mumbled under his breath.

"It's 21–17 in the final moments of the game," the announcers said. "Can the Rats break the back of the almighty Leopards with this last play?"

"No," Darnell answered for them. "Not happening."

Iako snapped the ball and his quarterback, Quartz Riley, stepped back. He flipped it to his running back who drove the ball toward the crowded line of scrimmage.

"That's it," Darnell sang. "It's over, baby!"

But Iako quickly juked his player and dove for the goal line. Both Iako and Darnell watched as the Rhode Island running back leaped over the pile of players and landed face first in the end zone.

"Nooooo!" Darnell shouted. "No—no—no!"

Iako smiled as the touchdown celebration began. His friend watched the screen in disbelief and shook his head.

"That's it, man," Darnell said. "That's it."

"No, hold on," Iako said. "There's still a minute left to play. You could run it down the field and—"

"No," Darnell said. "That's it for me. I'm officially retiring from this game."

Iako felt his heart sink. "What? No, c'mon, D. I didn't mean to—"

"You didn't mean to what, Iako?" Darnell asked, cutting off his friend. "You didn't mean to beat me with the worst team in the game? Seriously. I had Rick Armstrong playing. This shouldn't have happened!"

"Hey, I'm sorry, okay?" Iako said. "Let's play again. I'll, I don't know . . . ."

"Set the controller down and just let me play?" Darnell asked, then waved him off. "Hey, I'm not mad at you, seriously. It's just not fun for me anymore, you know? You're too good. You need some real competition."

CHAPTER 4

ONLINE OPPOSITION

Iako sat in his room alone. Darnell said he needed to get home since he was wiped out from practice. It felt more like an excuse. Iako hoped his friend wasn't mad for real.

I should've let him win, Iako thought to himself.

He looked at the game box. On the cover, running back Chuck Wembley from the Missouri Mammoths was shown running with the ball. Iako knew it probably bugged Darnell to be good at real football, but not great in the video game version.

Iako rolled over to his desk and opened up his laptop. He searched the internet a bit to learn about playing the game online.

Playing *FOOTBALL BLITZ: TURBO* against complete strangers wasn't something he'd ever thought about. He knew there were players online who were really good. But while he wanted some competition, Iako had heard people online could be pretty nasty.

Using the gift card he'd gotten for his birthday, Iako activated a three-month online membership. In his closet, he found the headset his cousin Matthias had given him for his Name Day last year.

Iako opened the box, pulled the headset out and fitted it onto his head. He felt like an airline pilot as he swung the microphone down in front of his mouth.

Iako then connected his console to the internet and went to the PLAY ONLINE option. He entered his online code and was asked to create an online username.

Iako stared at the screen, trying to think of something clever. He tried Wheelz5000, but that name was already taken. He considered IakotheJocko, but that just seemed dumb. After a handful of other unoriginal names, he settled on FreakYogurt224.

I'm Greek. We're known for yogurt. That plus my birthday should work, Iako thought, talking himself into it.

In a few moments the Blitz Board Online Matchup popped up on the screen. All sorts of user names scrolled by as they were paired off against others around the world.

Iako found the button on the screen that said LET'S PLAY, and hit START.

"Here goes nothing," Iako said to himself, prepared for the worst. He figured he could jump off and play against the computer if his online opponent wasn't any fun.

"Hey loser," a voice said over his headset. Iako jumped for a moment, not expecting to hear a voice right away. He looked at the screen and saw that he'd been matched against someone named AtomicSnotbox4026.

"You ready to cry through four quarters of pain and punishment?"

"Yeah," Iako said and shrugged. "Okay."

After selecting his team and players, the game started. The first two quarters were brutal. Snotbox easily drove his team up and down the field. Iako did his best to hold Snotbox back, but by the third quarter, he was behind by two touchdowns.

"Hey man," Snotbox sneered through his headset. "You're pretty terrible at this."

"You're not wrong," Iako said.

During the rest of the game, Snotbox kept talking trash. He said all kinds of nasty things Iako would never say out loud. Iako reached one hand to his headset and felt for the small volume dial. He spun it and, like magic, Snotbox's nasty comments faded away.

"Here we go," Iako said.

What happened next would've impressed Darnell, Luz, and probably the entire Carter Valley Crocs football team.

On the screen, Iako intercepted a long pass and ran it back over 80 yards for a touchdown. Then he scored a safety. He also sacked Snotbox's quarterback over and over again.

For fun, Iako turned the volume up to hear Snotbox screeching as his perfect game crumbled before him.

Iako turned the volume down again and focused on the game. In no time, he'd beaten his smack-talking opponent 42–21.

As the final score was displayed on screen, Iako said, "Hey man, good game."

Snotbox screamed but was cut off as Iako left the lobby to find another match-up.

Okay, he thought. *This isn't so bad.*

CHAPTER 5

NOT READY YET

Before Iako knew it, the first day of 7th grade had arrived. When he got to Carter Valley Middle School, he waved and shouted greetings to some of the kids he hadn't seen all summer. As he steered toward the access ramp next to the stairs, a familiar voice called out to him.

"Hey, Iako!" Luz cried, running over to him while clutching her backpack.

"*Hola*, new girl," Iako said, smiling. He waited for her to get closer before making his way up the ramp. "How was the rest of your summer?"

"*Bien, gracias*," Luz said with a nod. "Nice Spanish, by the way. The last week of summer was good. Lots of swimming practice and preparing myself for my first day here."

"You'll fit right in," Iako said. "Trust me. If a guy like me can do it, so can you."

"How about you?" Luz asked as they made their way to the front door. "Do anything exciting? Still playing your games?"

"Games?" Iako replied as he headed through the door. "Well, there's really only one game for me. But yeah, I play a lot of *FB:T*."

"So, what about that esports tournament? Thinking of entering?" Luz asked as they headed down the locker-lined hallway.

"Oh, no," Iako said. "It's not really for me. I don't like that kind of competition. Besides, there's also the—"

"Crowds, right." Luz finished for him. "Yeah, you said you're not a big fan of crowds."

"It's true," Iako said. "I think."

"You think?" Luz said, opening her locker and hanging her backpack inside. "Have you ever been in front of a crowd?"

"Well, yeah," Iako said. "We had to perform for choir last year. I felt like I was gonna barf."

"Ummm," Luz began, raising one eyebrow. "I'm pretty sure singing in front of people is a lot different than playing a game you're amazing at."

"Seriously, I'm not that good," Iako said.

"That's not what Darnell says," Luz replied. "You're too modest. You just don't want to admit how much you kick butt at it."

"Well, he retired from the game," Iako said. "Guess I beat him too many times."

"See?" Luz said, holding her hands up. "It's destiny, Iako."

"Hmm, maybe. I've actually started playing people online," Iako said, "since Darnell won't play anymore."

"Annnd . . .?"

Iako looked confused. "And what?"

"And how did it go? Have you lost yet?"

Iako rolled back and forth a few times and exhaled slowly.

"Not exactly," he replied.

"That's what I thought," Luz said. "Dude, you HAVE to get into this tournament."

Iako shook his head. "Nah. It's probably super expensive. Plus, there's the big crowd, and I only like to play for fun."

"Hey, being a champion can be fun," Luz said, closing her locker. "At least, that's what I hear."

Nearby, the bell rang, signaling the five-minute warning for period one.

"Whoa," Iako said. "I have to roll."

"Tournament," Luz said, staring intensely at Iako. "Tournament . . . tournament . . . ."

"Yeah, yeah," Iako said, rolling himself away. "I'll talk to you later!"

CHAPTER 6

CHAMPION CHARLES

Iako's first day at school was pretty easy.
The teachers spent most of the time letting
people introduce themselves. He knew almost
everyone already, but didn't have any classes
with Darnell.

After school, he saw Luz head toward the
pool area. Then he saw Darnell and a few
others walking toward the locker rooms for
football practice.

"Hey D!" Iako shouted. "Any chance you're
coming out of retirement? Maybe we can get
in a game of *FB:T* after practice?"

Darnell turned and put up his hands.
"I wish I could, man. But it's going to be
dinner time, then homework."

No one gets homework on the first day of school, Iako thought. *That sounds like an excuse.*

"Okay, no problem," Iako said. "Have a good practice, guys."

He watched as his best friend waved to him and then headed downstairs.

* * *

At dinner that night, Iako sat at the dinner table, deep in thought.

"You're barely touching your *bobota*," Mom said before forking up some more salad. "What's wrong, Iakovos?"

"Nothing," Iako replied, dipping his Greek cornbread in some creamy sauce and holding it in front of him. "I think Darnell's mad at me. He doesn't have time to hang out anymore."

"Darnell is a busy boy," Mom replied. "With the football and school work, it's harder for him to make time."

"I guess," Iako said. "Still stinks, though."

"He's your good friend," Mom replied. "He'll come around."

"I hope so," Iako said and took a bite.

* * *

That night, Iako powered up his console and jumped into an online session of *FB:T*. But it wasn't his favorite way to play. It wasn't the same as playing with your best friend, talking smack and laughing at stupid plays.

Iako squared off against a player named 12Boots and destroyed him. His next match was a close game, but he won by a field goal. None of the players were very friendly, and Iako turned down his headset volume to focus.

"Almost bedtime, Iakovos," Mom called from downstairs. "I don't want you playing that football all night."

Iako looked at the clock and knew he could get one last game in. "One more, Mom," Iako called.

In the BLITZ BOARD LOBBY, he was paired against ChampionCharles. Iako's eyes widened as he looked at his opponent's stats.

"Whoa. No losses," Iako whispered to himself. "We'll see about that."

As the game loaded, he heard a voice in the headset. "FreakYogurt? That's the best name you could come up with?"

"I'm Greek, so—" Iako began.

"Doesn't matter," Charles cut him off. "You'll lose. Just like everyone else."

Iako watched as Charles chose the New York Ninjas, one of the best teams in the league. To make things interesting, Iako chose the Texas Tarantulas, an average team.

The game was pretty challenging at first. Iako struggled to score against Charles's defense.

"You're terrible, Yogurt face," Charles hissed through the headset.

"Nice tackle," Iako replied. He badly wanted to return the nasty comment with one of his own but bit his tongue.

Near the end of the game, Iako had rallied to within a score. When he got the ball back, his quarterback made an incredible pass. If his receiver nabbed it, he could take the lead.

"You're not going to beat me, Freako," Charles blurted. "Not today, not ever."

Iako remained quiet as the pass landed perfectly in #80's hands. He turned, dodged Charles's linebacker and . . .

A message popped up on the screen:

ChampionCharles has left the game. Returning you to the lobby.

"What?" Iako cried as the screen cleared before his player could score.

This guy left the game before I had a chance to beat him! Iako thought. *What a poor loser!*

CHAPTER 7

VERY SNEAKY

Moving through the menus, Iako found the RECENT PLAYERS list. He clicked on it and found ChampionCharles at the top of the list. He selected Charles's profile and saw that his perfect record was still intact too: 278 wins, 0 losses.

"He didn't want to ruin his ridiculous winning streak," Iako said aloud, shaking his head. He scrolled down the player info page and found a quote in Charles's bio info:

THEEE BEST PLAYER YOU WILL EVER FACE! GET READY TO LOSE, LOSERZZZ!

Below that was a link to Charles's Chirper social media account.

Iako turned to his laptop and looked up ChampionCharles on Chirper. The header image showed a huge crowd and big electronic monitors in an indoor stadium. It looked like a football game was being played on the screen. In moments, Iako realized what he was looking at.

"ChampionCharles is a three-time *FB:T* esports champion," Iako whispered. "His name wasn't just for laughs."

Iako scrolled down and looked in disbelief at photos from previous tournaments. It showed an older kid holding a big trophy above his head. Charles had a big toothy smile and looked like he believed he was the king of the gridiron.

Just then an ad popped up for the upcoming esports *FB:T* tournament. Iako clicked on it out of curiosity. The tournament would be in November in Camden, New Jersey.

At least it's not too far away, Iako thought.

He looked up the location on MapIt! and discovered it was a less than an hour's drive from his house. He scrolled down to read more details. But then he saw there was a $250 entry fee.

"Forget that," Iako said, closing the window. He was fascinated by the idea of competing at the tournament. But between the big crowds and throwing away 250 bucks, he was out.

*   *   *

Three days later Luz approached him in the school lunchroom as he dumped the slop from his tray into the garbage.

"Hey stranger," Luz said, dumping her tray too. "Long time, no see."

"I'm no stranger than you," Iako replied with a smile.

"Very funny," she replied. "Do you have a minute? I want to show you something."

Iako put his tray on the return window and nodded. "Sure, I guess so."

Luz led him out of the lunchroom and down the hall to the library.

"Ookaaay," Iako said. "You know, I've been to the media center before. You didn't need to . . . ."

As Iako moved through the door, he saw Darnell sitting at a table near the front. He was obviously pretending to read a book.

"Hi, Iako," Darnell said.

"Okay," Luz said, taking a deep breath. "Now don't be mad."

"What's going on?" Iako demanded.

Luz looked at Darnell and he nodded for her to go on.

"Please don't be mad," Luz said. "But we got a bunch of people to pitch in and pay for your esports entry fee."

She handed him a printout that confirmed his registration to the big event. Iako's eyes widened in surprise.

"We all want you to compete," Darnell said. "You've kicked my butt too many times to count. You've got too much talent to waste it on me. Maybe it's time you kicked some national butts."

Iako shook his head in disbelief.

"Thanks, guys. It's really nice of you, but . . . ." Iako began. But then he looked at Luz and Darnell's smiling faces. In that moment, he thought about ChampionCharles and the awful things he'd said. He also remembered Charles's cheap move of leaving the game to prevent a loss.

"C'mon, Iako," Darnell said, growing impatient. "Say something, man."

"Uuuhhh . . . ooookay," Iako said with a smile. "I'm in."

CHAPTER 8

FACE THE CROWD

Iako spent the next month and a half training for the big esports event. Every day after school he headed to his room to finish his homework. Then he jumped online and played as many games as he could before bedtime.

Iako did everything he could to challenge himself. He picked bad teams on purpose. He made dumb plays to force himself to scramble and recover. When he wasn't holding a game controller, he stretched his fingers and squeezed stress balls to build up his hand strength.

Before he knew it, Iako and his mom were on their way to the Camden Sports Complex, just across the Delaware River. As they pulled into the parking lot, Iako's mom marveled at the building's size and the number of cars.

"Oh, St. Basil! This is a lot of madness for some video game football," she murmured.

Iako shrugged and pointed to a handicap accessible spot near the front of the building. "At least we get a good parking spot," he said.

Once inside, there were so many people that it was difficult for Iako and his mom to get around. Eventually, they found the registration table, signed some forms, and were told where to go for the tournament.

When they got to the door for the players, his mom gave him a hug and a kiss. "Good luck, Iakovos," she said, smiling. "I am sure you'll get all the points today."

Iako laughed. "Thanks, Mom. I'll try."

With that she went to find her seat in the stands. Meanwhile, Iako went to the waiting area with the rest of the *FOOTBALL BLITZ: TURBO* hopefuls.

*   *   *

As Iako watched the first few games, he couldn't help but look around. It felt and sounded like a real sporting event. There were giant monitors showing ten games at a time. Music boomed whenever a big play was made, and the crowds cheered and screamed for their favorite players.

He looked around for any familiar faces and saw only one.

ChampionCharles, he thought, remembering the guy's photo from his Chirper account.

Iako watched Charles shaking hands and taking selfies with some of his fans. He didn't bother smiling for the photos. Instead, he did his best to look tough. It was strange to see the guy standing right there in person.

A woman in a black and purple shirt came over to Iako. She wore a headset and held a data-pad.

"Are you FreakYogurt224?" she asked.

"I'm Iako," he replied, then realized she'd called him by his gamer name. "I mean, yes. Yes, I'm FreakYogurt."

"Okay, great," she said. "You're up for your first game."

Iako nodded and rolled forward.

"Great," he said. "Where's the ramp to get up on the stage?"

The woman looked up from her pad and made a face like she'd just seen a car accident.

"Ooooh," she said. "Oh, boy."

Iako looked around, trying to figure out how he was going to get onto the stage to compete. There didn't seem to be any other competitors in wheelchairs. The event organizers probably didn't think they'd need access for someone like him.

"Are you able to stand, or . . .?" the woman asked.

"No, not really," Iako said.

Just then he heard someone shouting from further up in the stands. He turned as Darnell and three other guys from the Carter Crocs football team approached. Luz followed close behind.

"Sit tight, Iako!" she shouted.

"We got you, champ," Darnell said.

Before Iako could say anything, all four of them lifted him up, wheelchair and all. The woman with the headset directed them to the stage and one of the playing stations beneath the enormous monitors.

"Thanks D," Iako said, feeling himself turn red. "Thanks guys."

"No need to thank us," Darnell said. "Now go win this thing!"

"We're behind you all the way," Luz said. "Show them who's boss, FreakYogurt!"

CHAPTER 9

THE BIG GAMES

As Darnell and his teammates set Iako down in front of his game station, he looked around. People filled nearly every seat in the giant Camden Sports Complex. It was a huge crowd, and he didn't like it.

"Win big, Iako," Darnell said. "Just pretend you're playing me!"

Iako managed a smile and fist-bumped his best friend. When they left, Iako looked nervously over at his opponent. It was an older guy in a backwards baseball cap. His gamer tag was Tuchdownz4Dayz106. Iako nodded at the player. He just stared hard at Iako and didn't nod back.

Great, Iako thought. *Another good sport.*

Iako took a deep breath, strapped on his headset, and picked up his controller. He listened as the officials explained the rules to the players. In the blink of an eye, it was time for kick-off.

Tuchdownz was on offense, and after just two plays, scored a touchdown. Iako cringed as he heard the crowd explode into excited cheers.

Then when he got the ball, Iako threw an interception that put him behind by two scores. By halftime, he was down 21–0.

I have to tune everyone out somehow, Iako thought.

When he played online at home, he could just turn down the volume on his headset. But that wouldn't work here. Instead, Iako turned the volume up so he could hear only the sounds of the game.

58

At that point, things changed. Iako came back strong in the third and fourth quarter. His defensive ends knocked over Tuchdownz's quarterback like he was made of straw. It was like a completely new player had entered the tournament.

Iako glanced over to see Tuchdownz leaning forward in his seat and shouting at the monitors. The tables had turned. Iako didn't let his opponent score another point. In the end, he won 35–21.

Tuchdownz tore off his headset and stomped off the stage. Meanwhile, Iako took off his headset to hear the crowd go absolutely wild. He looked down to see his friends on their feet cheering.

A guy could get used to this, Iako thought.

And he did. After four more decisive wins, Iako looked up at the bracket. Only two names remained:

FreakYogurt224 vs. ChampionCharles.

CHAPTER 10

LOSS FOR WORDS

The crowd was electric with excitement as the three-time champion took the stage. Charles walked over to Iako and held his hand out.

As Charles shook Iako's hand, he leaned in close. "I remember you and your dumb gamer name," he said. "I don't care if you're in a wheelchair or not, kid. I'm still going to kick your butt."

Iako just nodded and smiled. "Best of luck to you, Chuck," he said. "Too bad you can't jump offline if things don't go your way."

Just like their previous match, Charles selected the best team in the game, the New York Ninjas. Iako selected RANDOM to let the game pick his team for him. The crowd *Ooohed!* as the computer chose the Rhode Island Rats.

The worst team, Iako thought. *This'll be interesting.*

As the crowd's cheers and excitement rose to an almost deafening level, Iako turned his headphones up to drown out the crowd and anything Charles had to say. He felt the vibrations of the noise through his wheelchair, but that was it. Iako was in the zone.

When Charles' team kicked off, Iako's special teams player immediately ran it back for a touchdown. Iako's defense then put constant pressure on Charles's quarterback, forcing one incomplete pass after another. When Charles had to punt, Iako's team blocked it and ran it in for another score. In just two minutes, the score was already 14–0.

Iako saw Charles pounding his fists against the table. Things were not going well for him.

In the fourth quarter, the Rhode Island Rats forced Charles's quarterback back further and further down the field. Finally, they sacked him in the end zone to score a safety.

"He's cheating!" Charles shouted. "How can his team beat the Ninjas? It's impossible!"

Iako grinned. He replaced his headset and kept the pressure on. In the end, Iako won the championship with the weakest team in the game. And it wasn't even close. Final score: 54–0!

Charles stood up and threw his headset to the floor. Then he stormed off stage, screaming into a sea of cheering fans.

Darnell, Luz, and even Iako's mom found their way onto the stage to surround him. Sitting in the middle of a packed arena, Iako grinned from ear to ear.

Luz was right, he thought. *Being a champion IS fun.*

* * *

Two days later, Iako and Darnell were back in his bedroom, playing their first game of *FB:T* in months.

The two friends picked average teams. They laughed and shouted at bad plays and even worse calls from the refs. At the end of the fourth quarter, Darnell fired a long pass downfield.

Amazingly, Darnell's receiver leaped up to catch the pass. Iako's defender dove at the receiver's feet but missed.

"And that . . . is . . . GAME!" Darnell shouted as his player scored. He stood up and did an end zone dance. "Finally!"

Iako smiled. "Good game, D," he said. "You got me."

Darnell shook his head. "I know you let me win."

"No way," Iako said.

"Doesn't matter," Darnell said, reaching into his pocket and pulling out a folded brochure. "A deal's a deal."

"All right," Iako said. "Let me see."

Darnell handed the paper over to Iako. On it were boys and girls in wheelchairs playing football.

"They have co-ed teams, boy's teams, girl's teams," Darnell said, nodding to the brochure. "Everything."

Iako looked it over. Everyone looked like they were having fun throwing around a real football. There were players with several degrees of ability. It didn't look like it mattered.

"Are there crowds there?" Iako asked.

"Oh, c'mon!" Darnell cried. "Not this excuse again. Of course there are crowds there."

"Okay," Iako said with a smile. "I'm in."

MORE ABOUT ESPORTS AND FOOTBALL VIDEO GAMES

- The first real video game competition took place at Stanford University in October, 1972. Students there competed in a game called *Spacewar*. The grand prize was a year-long subscription to *Rolling Stone* magazine.

- The earliest football video game was called FTBALL, created in 1965. It was played on a computer.

- The biggest esports game is Dota 2. The name stands for Defense of the Ancients 2 and is a multiplayer online battle arena (MOBA) game.

- The John Madden Football franchise is the longest running series of football video games in history. It has been going strong for more than 30 years, with more than 40 titles in the series.

- *Madden 21* introduced a new game mode called The Yard. It showcases teams of six players competing against each other in a "backyard" football competition. The new mode was first used in an esports event in March, 2021.

- Esports teams usually practice together for 8 hours a day, 7 days a week. That's longer than a full-time 40 hour per week job. Many players also practice on their own time after that.

- A research study showed that during esports competitions, players had heart rates around 160–180 beats per minute. That's about the same as a person's heart rate after running a mile as fast as they can.

- Being an esports athlete isn't just about sitting in a chair and playing video games all day. The best competitors get physical exercise to train their body and mind, and to sharpen their reflexes. Stretching and upper body exercises help keep esports athletes healthy!

TALK ABOUT IT

1. Why does Iako say he's "not that good" at playing FOOTBALL BLITZ: TURBO? Why would he think he's bad at the game when he wins every time?

2. Are Luz and Darnell too pushy when they say Iako should compete in the esports tournament? How would you react if your friends pushed you to do something you didn't feel comfortable with?

3. Early in the book, Iako says he doesn't like crowds. Why do you think this is? Is he shy, or embarrassed, or nervous? Do you think it has something to do with being in a wheelchair?

WRITE ABOUT IT

1. What would happen if Darnell hadn't "retired" from playing against Iako in *FOOTBALL BLITZ: TURBO*? Would he eventually be able to challenge Iako? Write an action scene showing Darnell finally beating Iako in the game.

2. ChampionCharles lost the esports tournament. Write a scene about what Charles did after storming off the stage. What would he think of getting beaten by a guy in a wheelchair who played the worst team? What do you think he'd do next after losing so badly to Iako?

3. Iako agrees to try playing wheelchair football after making a bet with Darnell. Write a few paragraphs about how Iako does in his new sport after playing video game football for so long.

GLOSSARY

bobota (buh-BOH-tuh)—a type of sweet cornbread made in Greece

esports (EE-sports)—competitive tournaments that feature video games and professional gamers

handicap accessible (HAN-dee-kap ak-SES-uh-buhl)—alterations made so that a person with a disability can use something, such as a special parking space or a ramp next to stairs

line of scrimmage (LINE UHV SKRIM-ij)—an imaginary line running across a football field that marks where the football lies at the beginning of a play

muscular dystrophy (MUSS-kyoo-lur DIS-truh-fee)—a disease where a person's muscles gradually weaken and waste away

Name Day (NAYM DAY)—a tradition in some European countries in which a person celebrates their given name, similar to a birthday celebration

safety (SAYF-tee)—when a player is tackled behind his own goal line; the defense is awarded two points and the ball

ABOUT THE AUTHOR

Thomas Kingsley Troupe is the author of a big ol' pile of books for kids. He's written about everything from ghosts to Bigfoot to 3rd grade werewolves. He even wrote a book about dirt. When he's not writing or reading, he gets plenty of exercise, plays video games, and remembers sacking quarterbacks while on his high school football team. Thomas lives in Woodbury, Minnesota with his two sons.

ABOUT THE ILLUSTRATOR

Fran Bueno is a comic artist with over 25 years of experience. He graduated in Fine Arts from the Complutense University of Madrid and has worked on illustrations for pamphlets, advertisements, children's books, and young adult comics. Fran also teaches traditional inking and graphic skills at the O Garaxe Hermético Professional School of Comics. He lives in Santiago de Compostela, Spain.

JAKE MADDOX eSPORTS
READ THEM ALL!

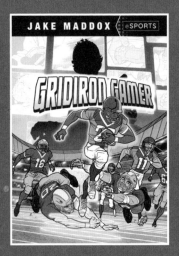